Elfinbright

The Tale of the Forever Present

Written by

JOHN V. TOCCO

Illustrated by

NANCY VELICK SMITH

Favorite Uncle Books

www.favoriteunclebooks.com

LCCN 2001117777
ISBN 0-9711665-0-1

Favorite Uncle Books LLC, North American Division
23228 Lawrence, Suite 1A, Dearborn, MI, 48128-1230
www.favoriteunclebooks.com

Artist's Note: The illustrations were created with art markers,
colored pencils and acrylic paints on 100 pound bristol board.

Design direction and Interior layout by James V. Tocco, Grosse Pointe Woods, MI.

Printed in Korea by Bookability, Inc., Davison, MI.

To *Janice for her vivid verbs;*

Renee for her gentle and honest editing;

*The 1998–99 seventh grade class at
Gull Lake Middle School for reminding me about Santa;*

Beth for the great inspirational breakfast;

*Paul for his support and for being a good egg
about ending up on the cutting room floor;*

*Nancy for giving the dream shape, color, texture,
and a teddy bear; and*

*Mom and Dad for making sure that Santa visited
us every year.*

— JOHN V. TOCCO

To *John for the opportunity to realize a dream;*

Patricia, who will always be in my heart;

My parents for nurturing the artist in me;

Kenneth and Sherman for simply being; and

Danny for being my everything.

—NANCY VELICK SMITH

Elfinbright

The Tale of the Forever Present

he letter to Santa was not quite finished. One or two final touches, color the envelope, add a stamp, and mail it off.

Just then James had a thought. "What about the elves?" he asked his brother Jacob.

"What about them?" replied Jacob.

"Well, they must work hard to make all those toys. Should we thank the elves by inviting them over on Christmas Eve?"

"Do you think Santa would mind?" Jacob asked.

"No way," said James emphatically.

Jacob looked over the letter. "I think there's enough room," he reported. At the end of the letter Jacob added a P.S:

> *"Santa, please invite the elves to come with you to our house on Christmas Eve. We want to thank them for working so hard at making toys for us. We'll leave cookies and milk out for them—right next to yours!"*

Jacob sealed the envelope, and the boys hurried outside, bounding through the snowdrifts to the mailbox down the street.

Santa, his reading glasses perched precariously on the end of his nose, leaned back in his overstuffed easy chair, rubbed his eyes, and sighed. "Well, that should do it," he said quietly to himself, "I'm finally done checking the list."

"Not quite, dear." Mrs. Claus stood in the doorway of Santa's study, holding one last letter. Freya, the tiniest of the elves, grasped Mrs. Claus' other hand.

"Ah! Sweetheart! And Freya!" Santa exclaimed. "Come give Santa a hug." Freya darted across the room with the letter and jumped onto Santa's lap. Her little arms barely reached around Santa's thick neck. "And who is this from, my little elf-niece?"

"It's from Jacob and James."

A smile of relief flashed across Santa's face. "I was worried that they had forgotten about me," Santa whispered earnestly.

"Oh, Uncle Santa, they would never do that!" Freya replied, playfully tugging on his long white beard.

BOWLATHON

1741-1745 | 1746-1750

1751-1755 | 1756-1760

1761-1765 | 1766-1770 | 1771-1775

SANTA
NORTH POLE

JAMES JACOB

ZOE
TOMMY
JANICE
JOHN
KATY

BRUCE
GRETEL
CHARLIE
GINA
JIMMY
DEANN
DANIEL
PATRICIA
CARL
ANINA
KENNY
BETH
KYLE
SUZY
HARRY
DEBORAH
SHERMAN
ANN
PAUL
JI

LILLIAN
KELLY
EDDIE
MARIE
RUSS
CARMELA
PAMELA
MATT
NATALIE
TONY
MICHAEL
ASHLEY
DEBBIE
HENRY
ELIZABETH
TERRY
SARAH
JOSEPH
RACHE
BOB
M
W
JI

Santa beamed
as he read the letter.
Then, when he read
the P.S., his bushy eyebrows
shot up in surprise.
"Hmmm," he said thoughtfully,
slowly stroking his beard.

"It's time for bed, Santa! Christmas Eve is almost here, and you need your rest!" Mrs. Claus reminded Santa, wagging a finger at him.

"Auntie's right," agreed Freya, imitating the finger waggle, an exaggerated scowl on her face.

"Yes, dears," Santa replied, as he padded off to bed, still clutching the letter from Jacob and James.

On Christmas Eve day SantaHall was abuzz with activity. Hundreds of elves dashed about in a frenzy to finish their final tasks for Santa's trip. In the center of the cavernous hall, on a raised platform and under a flood of brilliant lights, rested Santa's grand and glorious sleigh.

The reindeer were harnessed, groomed, and fed; presents were wrapped, beribboned, and packed; and the sleigh bells were cleaned, polished, and buffed.

Santa and Mrs. Claus, arm in arm, climbed the platform. Mrs. Claus patted Donner on the nose as she admired the sleigh.

"Oh, how lovely!" she exclaimed. Many of the elves, wide grins on their faces, blushed.

Santa, slowly circling the sleigh and nodding his head in approval, finally remarked, "My ride's looking mighty fine, *mighty* fine!"

After one last peck on the cheek from his wife, Santa climbed aboard the sleigh, cleared his throat, and commenced his yearly thank-you speech.

"Well my little elf-friends, once again you've done an excellent job. I am grateful for your hard work, as are all the children I will visit." The elves cheered.

Santa reached into the pocket of his bright red coat and retrieved the letter from Jacob and James. "Oh yes, and one other thing." Santa held the letter aloft for all to see. "Jacob and James have invited all the elves over to their house tonight for milk and cookies. So, if you would like to go, climb aboard!"

The elves were dumbfounded. Was Santa serious? Couldn't be. Go with Santa to deliver presents? No way. Milk and cookies on Christmas Eve? Yeah, right. They traded puzzled glances and waited. Finally Freya broke the silence.

"Rooooad triiiiip!" she shouted at the top of her lungs. Her voice reverberated throughout SantaHall.

Amidst wild cheering, Freya and several elves scrambled onto the sleigh.

Santa called out to the reindeer, each in turn, urging them to start their long journey.

Donner
hesitated,
and looked
back at Freya.
She glanced about to
make sure the elves were
settled, gave Donner a "thumbs up," and shouted,
"Good to go!" The reindeer rose into the air,
effortlessly drawing the
sleigh through the open skylight
of SantaHall and into the starry
North Pole sky.

All through the night,
at the gentle urgings of Santa, the reindeer
dipped and turned and soared, landed
and waited patiently, and again took flight.
The elves nervously craned their necks
over the sides of the sleigh, staring wide-eyed
at the wondrous world below.

Suddenly Santa called out,
"Rooftop HO! Good Donner!"
Off in the distance a house was
nestled cozily behind a grove
of tall evergreens.
Donner guided the reindeer to an expert
landing alongside the chimney.

"This is Jacob's and James' house,"
Santa whispered. "You must be very quiet; we don't want
to wake the boys." Santa, his bright red toy bag slung over
his shoulder, gracefully slid down the chimney.

Then, one after another, the elves followed. They tumbled out of the fireplace in a heap, some ending up on their heads, others flat on their backs, all of them giggling hysterically.

"Hush!" cautioned Santa. The elves covered their mouths with tiny gloved hands, but the giggling continued.

Santa rolled his eyes at the elves, and then set to work placing the gaily-wrapped gifts under the Christmas tree.

Santa discovered a plate of chocolate chip cookies and a pitcher of cold milk on a table next to the tree. "It looks like the boys spent all day baking. Well, go ahead, have a cookie or two. Jacob and James will be disappointed if you come all this way and don't take advantage of their hospitality!" The elves huddled around the milk and cookies, and whispered among themselves.

"Well, we must be on our way!" Santa finally said. "We've spent too much time here, and we still have a long journey ahead of us."

"We want to leave the boys one more present," replied Freya.

"Look under the tree," pleaded Santa, glancing nervously at the clock on the fireplace mantel. He hadn't been this far behind schedule in 500 years. "You want to leave more?"

"Yes," said Freya, quietly but firmly. "We want to give Jacob and James a special present—a *forever* present."

Santa stared wide-eyed at Freya. "A forever present is a serious matter. Are you certain you want to do this, little elf-niece?"

Freya and all the elves nodded their heads vigorously.

"OK, OK, but be quick about it!" cried Santa, as loudly as he dared.

The elves, their soft-soled boots soundless on the thick carpet, darted out the front door and disappeared among the grove of evergreens. Santa glanced at the clock again, rolled his eyes, and sighed.

After a scrumptious Christmas dinner, long after the presents were opened, Jacob and James helped clear the table and wash the dishes. They ran to the Christmas tree to play with their toys, but something out the front window caught their attention. Noses pressed against the windowpane, the boys stared in amazement at the grove of evergreens. "Awesome!" they exclaimed in unison, sprinting outside, zipping up their coats as they bounded through the snowdrifts.

And what a glorious sight it was!
The evergreens, usually a deep,
dark green in the winter night, were
speckled with thousands and thousands
of tiny, twinkling lights. The trees looked
like tall, graceful spires of crystal,
blanketed with sparkling diamonds.
     "Hey! There are no electrical cords!"
exclaimed Jacob, puzzlement in his voice.

It began to snow. The snowflakes,
  like the trees, glimmered brilliantly, swirling
this way and that, then gently flittered to earth
  like millions of fireflies resting after a long journey.
Laughing, the boys spun in dizzying circles,
arms outspread, until their coats and hats and faces
  were covered with fluffy, glowing flakes.

Jacob and James
built a snowman
that glowed like a full moon
on a clear winter's evening.

They tossed snowballs that
soared through the glittering flakes,
like fiery comets streaking through
the heart of the Milky Way.

The boys played among the dazzling trees for many hours. Finally exhausted, they trudged back toward the house. Just then, Jacob discovered a small note on one of the trees. He read it aloud to James.

Dearest Jacob and James,

Thank you so much for the thoughtful invitation. We loved the cookies and milk. We will forever hold in our hearts this most special night. So you always remember our love and gratitude, please accept our gift of the Elfinbright Grove for you to enjoy every Christmas Night.

Forever Yours in Christmas,
Freya and Santa's Elves

At the front door
the boys gazed
at Elfinbright Grove
once more, and
watched the lights slowly dim
like thousands of tiny sunsets.
Although they couldn't
be sure, they thought
they heard, faintly
and far off in the
distance, the jingling of
dozens of tiny bells.
When the boys closed the door
the snow ceased, and the
evergreens turned once
again to a deep, dark green.

As the elves had promised, the present of Elfinbright Grove was truly forever. For Jacob and James, and their children, and their grandchildren, and so on ever after, gathered among the evergreens every Christmas evening to build snowmen, sing carols, and bask in the glow of a million dazzling lights.

The invitation, too, was truly forever. For Freya and the elves remembered always the generous spirit and the thoughtfulness of two boys named Jacob and James.